Mrs Klavens

GAN ISRAEL DAY CAMP

A PROJECT OF CHABAD-LUBAVITCH OF W. MONMOUTH COUNTY

ב״ה

This gift is awarded to:

Rachel Goldfarb

for her achievement in
Tzivos Hashem.

Elul 5754
August 1994

Rabbi Boruch & Tova Chazanow
Camp Directors

בס"ד

HERSHEL'S HOUSEBOAT

Written & Illustrated by

MICHOEL MUCHNIK

Revised Color Edition
Published and Copyrighted © 1984
by Merkos L'inyonei Chinuch, Inc.
770 Eastern Parkway
Brooklyn, New York 11213
(718) 774-4000 / 493-9250

ISBN 0-8266-0354-8

Color by Barry Grossman

Printed in the United States of America

In honor of the

"Year Dedicated to Torah Education"

This book was written with the hope that every Jewish child will make this world a dwelling place for G-d, through the observance of Torah and Mitzvos.

NE day Mendel and Rachel decided to visit their friend, Hershel the Housebuilder. He was a wonderful carpenter, and had built many of the houses in the town where Mendel and Rachel lived.

They awoke early in the morning, said the "Shema", ate breakfast, and off they went to look for Hershel. They walked down the long street, hoping to find Hershel at work building a new house.

When Mendel and Rachel came to Shimon's Shoestore, they opened the door and peeked in. "Hello," said Shimon. "Do you need new shoes?"

"No, thank you," said Mendel. "We're quite happy with the ones we have. We would just like to know if you have seen Hershel today."

"No, I haven't seen him," answered Shimon.

"Well, thank you anyway," said Mendel. They continued to ask their neighbors, but no one seemed to know where to find Hershel.

"I don't know," said Faygie, the Flower Lady.

"I don't know, either," said Sholom the Student, carrying his Gemorra on his way to Yeshiva.

"I don't think we'll ever find Hershel today," said Mendel sadly.

"Let's go visit Chaya the Challah Lady, instead," suggested Rachel.

"That's a good idea," said Mendel. "Maybe her husband, Meyer the Miller, will let us help grind some flour."

It was very busy at the mill, but Meyer the Miller greeted Mendel and Rachel with a happy face. Chaya was inside, baking challahs. "Why, hello!" said Meyer. "What a nice surprise. What brings you here on such a nice sunny day?"

"We are looking for Hershel. We want to watch him build a new house, but we can't find him anywhere," said Mendel.

"Well, how hard are you trying?" asked Meyer.

"I guess not very hard," said Mendel.

"If you will look hard enough, then you will surely find," said Meyer. He was very wise.

Suddenly, they heard all kinds of loud noises coming from outside, beneath the window. "CLANK CLANK BONK BONK TINK TINK NIZZLE WOOP!"

"What's that?" asked Chaya, rushing to the window.

"Maybe it's raining," said Rachel.

"Who is making that noise down there?" called Chaya.

"Why, it's me," said a voice.

"Who's ME?" cried Chaya.

"Hershel the Housebuilder!"

"What are you doing in the river?" asked Chaya.

"I'm building my new house."

"In the RIVER?" cried Meyer. "Let's go outside on the porch and take a look." Meyer, Chaya, Mendel and Rachel walked out onto the porch and looked down. Sure enough, there was Herhsel the Housebuilder, standing on the roof of a new house.

"My goodness," said Chaya. "We're so sorry that your new house fell into the river."

"No, no," said Hershel. "This house didn't fall in the river. This house FLOATS on the river! It is a houseboat!"

"Why are you building a houseboat?" asked Rachel.

"For Hashem (G-d) to live in, of course," said Hershel. "Come down to the dock and I will tell you all about it."

They all walked down to see Hershel's new houseboat. Hershel then explained a wonderful idea from the Torah. "The reason that Hashem created the whole wide world is so that people can make it the kind of place where He will want to live."

"How can we do that?" asked Mendel and Rachel.

"By learning all the good teachings of the Torah and by doing Mitzvos wherever you are, even in a houseboat. Would you like to take a ride with me down the river for a while?"

"Oh, yes!" said Mendel and Rachel together.

"See how many Mitzvos you can do on the houseboat," said Chaya. "Then Hashem will surely ride along with you."

"I know a Mitzvah we can do," said Rachel. "Let's go visit Aunt Tovah! She doesn't feel well today. Her house is on the riverbank. If we call her from Hershel's houseboat, maybe she will feel better."

"That's a fine idea," said Hershel. They waved to Meyer the Miller and Chaya the Challah Lady and sailed off down the river. When they came to Aunt Tovah's house, they called out, "Aunt Tovah! Aunt Tovah!" Soon they saw her face appear at the window.

"Who is calling me from the river?"

"It's us," answered Rachel, and Hershel beeped his horn.

"Well, look who it is! What a wonderful surprise!" said Aunt Tovah, and she began to laugh.

"How are you feeling today?" called Mendel.

"Much better now, Baruch Hashem. Thank you so much for coming to cheer me up. Bye now!"

A little further down the river Mendel noticed his friend, Berel, sitting alone on the bank. "There is Berel," said Mendel, "but he looks very sad. Let's invite him to join us in doing Mitzvos."

"That will be a Mitzvah in itself," said Hershel, "the Mitzvah of Ahavas Yisroel, loving another Jew as oneself." He drove the boat up to the shore. They called to Berel to join them.

"Welcome aboard," said Mendel. "Wouldn't you like to help us make Hershel's Houseboat a place in which Hashem will want to be?"

"Yes, but I can't think of anything special that I can do," said Berel sadly.

Mendel, Rachel and Hershel thought very, very, VERY hard about what Berel could do. "I don't really know," said Mendel.

"Neither do I," said Hershel.

"Can you sing?" asked Rachel.

"Yes, I can sing," answered Berel. "I know! I'll sing about the greatness of Hashem!"

"Why, how wonderful!" said Hershel. "Our Father Avraham was the first Jew to tell everyone that there is only One G-d, and how great He is. G-d must have loved Avraham very, very much."

Berel began to sing his song. "Hashem is here, Hashem is there, Hashem is truly everywhere."

"Wait, no one can hear you," said Hershel. "Take my horn and sing into it. Then people will hear you."

Berel sang his song through the horn.

"HASHEM IS HERE,
  HASHEM IS THERE,

HASHEM IS TRULY
  EVERYWHERE.

UP, UP, DOWN, DOWN, RIGHT,
  LEFT, ALL AROUND,

HERE, THERE, AND
  EVERYWHERE,

THAT'S WHERE HE CAN BE
  FOUND!"

At first, only a few people could be seen looking out of their windows to see where the song was coming from. "Sing louder, sing louder!" cried Rachel.

"HASHEM IS HERE, HASHEM IS THERE, HASHEM IS TRULY EVERYWHERE!!!"

Berel's song was so loud that all the people along the river opened their windows wide and looked to see who was singing such a wonderful song. Everyone was so happy to see the houseboat and to hear Berel singing his song. They all cheered and clapped along.

"I'm so glad that we asked you to come along with us," said Mendel to Berel. "Look how happy you have made everyone." Berel was very happy now, too.

"Let's go," said Hershel. "The time has come for me to take all of you home." Hershel steered the houseboat to the dock near the end of the street where Mendel and Rachel lived. "Come visit again soon," Hershel said.

"Thank you for the ride, Hershel," said Berel. "Next time, may I bring my brother and sister, too?"

"Why, of course," said Hershel. "Bye, bye now. Have a good day!"

"Bye, bye," said Mendel and Rachel. Together they all walked home.